Starry Forest Books, Inc. • P.O. Box 1797, 217 East 70th Street, New York, NY 10021 • Starry Forest® is a registered trademark of Starry Forest Books, Inc. • Text and Illustrations © 2020 by Starry Forest Books, Inc. • This 2020 edition published by Starry Forest Books, Inc. • All rights reserved. No part of this publication may be reproduced, stored in a retrieval system, or transmitted in any form or by any means (including electronic, mechanical, photocopying, recording, or otherwise) without prior written permission from the publisher. • ISBN 978-1-946260-28-4 • Manufactured in Huizhou City, Guangdong Province, China • Lot #: 2 4 6 8 10 9 7 5 3 1 • 04/20

CLASSIC STORIES

Alice's Adventures in Wonderland

Lewis Carroll

retold by Saviour Pirotta

illustrated by Amerigo Pinelli

Starry Forest Books

Alice was falling asleep next to her sister when she spied a white rabbit.

"Oh dear," cried the Rabbit. "I'm late." He disappeared into a hole at the base of a tree.

A talking rabbit? thought Alice. *How curious!* She leapt up, followed the White Rabbit, and leaned into the hole.

Alice tumbled down, down, down, past shelves and cupboards until she landed, *thump*, in a long hall.

Alice ran after the White Rabbit, who disappeared around a corner. *How shall I find my way out?* Alice wondered.

She saw a beautiful rose garden, but the door was locked. She was too big to fit through it anyway.

Much to Alice's surprise, a table appeared. There was
a little key on it, and a bottle labelled: **DRINK ME.**

Alice drank, and soon she'd shrunk so that she was just the right size to fit through the door. But, bother! Alice had left the key on the table and now she could not reach it. Alice noticed a cake with the words **EAT ME** on it. She ate some cake and . . .

. . . *grew*! Poor Alice was so confused by all the shrinking and growing that she began to cry tremendous tears. Just then, the White Rabbit bolted past Alice so fast that he dropped his gloves and his fan. Alice used the fan to cool her hot, tear-streaked face. Before she knew it, she had fanned herself small again.

Alice jumped, trying to reach the key on the table, and *splash!*
She fell into a salty pool of her own tears.

I wish I hadn't cried so much while I was big, she thought.

As she swam, everything changed. The hall with the little door and the table with the key on it vanished completely. She was in the woods.

Alice clambered up the muddy bank out of the pool of tears. She saw other animals climbing out, too.

"We should run races to dry off," suggested the Dodo.

They all ran around in a big circle, droplets flying off them
as they ran.

"Are there prizes?" asked the Eaglet when they stopped running.

Alice thought this was odd; they had only been running to dry off.

"I have almonds we can use as prizes," Alice said.

"But *you* deserve a prize, too," said the Duck.

"I only have a thimble left," said Alice.

"That will do," said the Dodo, giving Alice her own thimble as a prize!

"Goodbye, Alice," called the creatures as they ran off.

The White Rabbit sped by. Alice chased him but could not keep up. Instead, she bumped into a towering mushroom. A caterpillar lounged on it, smoking a water pipe. "Whoooo are YOU?" he asked.

"I'm not sure," admitted Alice. "I keep growing bigger and smaller. I'd like to be my *normal* size."

"If you eat one side of the mushroom, it will make you smaller," drawled the Caterpillar. "The other side will make you bigger."

Alice nibbled pieces of the mushroom until she was her normal height.

Then she met a large cat. "What kind of cat are you?" she asked.

"I'm a Cheshire Cat," the Cat replied, grinning from whisker to whisker.

"Which way is the rose garden, please?" asked Alice.

"To the right," said the Cat, pointing its tail, "lives a Mad Hatter." Then the Cat pointed its tail left and said, "And to the left lives a March Hare. Either will help you."

"Thank you," Alice said.

"You're welcome," said the Cat. Then it grew fainter and fainter, until only its grin was left.

I've seen a cat without a grin, thought Alice, *but I've never seen a grin without a cat!*

Alice had not gone very far when she came to a table set for tea. *How lovely!* thought Alice. The Mad Hatter and the March Hare were sitting at the table with a sleeping dormouse between them.

"No room! No room!" cried the Hare as Alice approached.

"Don't be silly. There's plenty of room," said Alice, sitting down.

"Why is a raven like a writing desk?" the Hatter asked Alice.

"I don't know," said Alice.

"Neither do I," said the Hatter.

The Hare shook his watch. "Two days wrong," he groaned. "I knew rubbing it with butter wouldn't fix it." He dipped the watch in his tea.

Neither the Hatter nor the Hare made any sense.

I'll have to ask someone else the way to the rose garden, thought Alice.

Walking on, Alice saw a door in a tree. She opened it and crawled through. *I'm in the rose garden at last,* she thought happily.

"Good day, Miss," the three gardeners greeted Alice.

"I beg your pardon," said Alice. "May I ask why you are painting white roses red?"

"The Queen of Hearts only likes *red* roses," whispered a gardener nervously. "If she finds out that we planted white roses by mistake, she'll chop off our heads!"

"Dear me!" said Alice. "The Queen sounds dreadful!"

Suddenly trumpets blasted a loud fanfare. "The Queen is coming," gasped the gardeners, hastily hiding the red paint.

The Queen squinted at Alice. "Do you play croquet?" she asked.

"Yes, your majesty," answered Alice, curtseying politely.

"Then come along," the Queen commanded.

It was a very strange croquet match.
The balls scurried away, the mallets curled,
and sometimes the wickets stood up!

"Enough!" ordered the Queen, flinging her mallet aside. "Time for the trial."

"What trial?" asked Alice.

No one replied. Alice followed the crowd to the courtroom and sat with the Hare, Dormouse, and Hatter. Guards dragged in a terrified Knave of Hearts.

"Read the accusation," said the King of Hearts.
The White Rabbit read:

> The Queen of Hearts The Knave of Hearts
> She made some tarts He stole the tarts
> All on a summer's day. And took them clean away.

"Off with his head!" roared the Queen.

The White Rabbit said, "My first witness is Alice."

"But I don't know anything," bleated Alice.

"Off with HER head!" bellowed the Queen.

"Nonsense!" said Alice hotly. The angrier she felt, the taller she grew. "You are nothing but a pack of cards."

At that, the whole pack of cards flew at her, pelting her in the face.

"Alice, wake up," called a gentle voice. Alice opened her eyes.
She was back on the riverbank.

"Are you all right?" her sister asked.

"I'm fine—*now*," said Alice, laughing and brushing leaves off her dress. "But *wait* till I tell you: I've had *such* a curious dream."